D0602345

HEATHCLIFF®

Heathcliff's Night Before Christmas

by Robb Lawrence
illustrated by Steve Smallwood

WATERMILL PRESS
HEATHCLIFF Copyright © 1988 McNaught Syndicate, Inc. All rights reserved.
Published by Watermill Press under License by Marvel Books, a New World Company.
ISBN 0-8167-1559-9

What excitement! It was the night before Christmas at the Nutmegs' house. And there was so much to do to get ready for Christmas day.

Outside, the cold wind blew and the snow came down in big, white flakes. But inside, it was warm and cozy. Grandpa built a fire in the fireplace. Grandma made steaming cups of hot chocolate.

"Now it's time to decorate the tree," said Grandpa. They took out colored ornaments, Christmas balls, twinkling lights, and popcorn strings for the tree.

"What fun!" thought Heathcliff.

"Hey, Heathcliff—" shouted Iggy. "Put those down!"

"The tree looks great," said Grandma when it was all decorated.

"One more thing to do," said Iggy. He climbed on Grandpa's shoulders to put the silver star on the very top of the tree.

"Now let's put all the presents under the tree," said Grandma.

They all brought out presents to put under the tree. Heathcliff wanted to help, too. "Wow! I'll bet this is a big box of cat food for me!" he thought. "Yum!"

"Hey, Heathcliff—" shouted Iggy. "Put that down!!"

"Let's sing some Christmas carols," said Grandma. "That will really give us Christmas spirit."

They began to sing.

"Oh boy," thought Heathcliff. "I love to sing!"

He opened his mouth wide, tossed back his head, and began to sing, too, as loudly as he could—which was quite loud!

"What's that awful noise?" asked Grandma.

"Is someone stepping on Heathcliff's tail?" asked Grandpa.

"No. He's singing!" cried Iggy. "Heathcliff—stop that right now!"

"Oh no!" cried Iggy. "Look, Grandpa, Grandma! Look at what Heathcliff did!"

"Uh oh," thought Heathcliff. "I think I may be in trouble now."

"Heathcliff ate all the Christmas cookies we baked!" cried Iggy. "And he ate the popcorn off the tree. And he ate the milk and cookies we left on the mantel for Santa Claus! Now Santa Claus probably won't even come here!"

Poor Iggy. He was very, very sad.

Heathcliff looked sad, too. "I can't do anything right around here," he thought. "I guess Christmas isn't for cats."

He decided he had to go away so the Nutmegs could enjoy their holiday. Out into the cold, snowy night he went. The snow froze his paws, and the icy winds made him shiver. "Maybe Sonja is home," he thought, feeling cold and miserable.

He knocked on her door.

"Heathcliff, what on earth are you doing out this late?" Sonja shouted. "You woke me up! Now go back where you belong!"

She slammed the door in Heathcliff's face.

Heathcliff wandered on.

"Oh no!" he thought. "Here come Spike and Muggsy! What are they doing out on Christmas Eve? Just looking for trouble, I guess."

Heathcliff guessed right. Spike started to growl. Then he started to bark. Then he started to chase Heathcliff.

He chased him into a big pile of wet snow.

"Ha! Ha!" laughed Muggsy. "Look at that! Spike made a snowman!"

Heathcliff walked on. The snow came down faster. The wind blew harder. He was very sad.

Suddenly, he heard a loud *plop*. A big sack dropped onto a pile of snow. "What could that be?" Heathcliff wondered.

He ran up and looked inside the sack. It was filled with toys and all kinds of presents. It must have fallen from Santa's sleigh.

Heathcliff began whistling as loudly as he could. "Santa, come back! Come back!" Would Santa hear his whistles?

Santa's sleigh swooped softly down for a landing. The sound of jingle bells filled the air. The reindeers pawed the snow, eager to fly again.

Santa walked over to Heathcliff. His beard was even whiter than the snow. His black eyes glowed merrily like small coals.

"Thank you for rescuing my sack full of toys," Santa said to the surprised cat. "There would be a lot of disappointed boys and girls if it weren't for you, Heathcliff. Would you like to come with me and help me deliver these presents?"

Santa didn't have to ask twice. Heathcliff leaped into the sleigh!

Up, up they flew, up over the trees, over the houses.

"I can sure use a helper," Santa told Heathcliff. "There's so much to do before morning."

"This is exciting!" thought Heathcliff. He had never flown before. He had never been this high up. He had never even climbed a tall tree!

"What fun!" Heathcliff thought. Then he made one big mistake. He looked down!

Ullllp!

Heathcliff followed Santa down the chimneys. What a thrilling night!

He helped Santa deliver the presents.

And he helped eat all the treats and goodies that kids had left for Santa.

Santa couldn't eat them all, could he?!

It was nearly morning when Heathcliff returned home. He was very tired—and *very* full!

He wanted to sleep. But Iggy was already waking up. It was time to open the Christmas presents.

There were presents under the tree for everyone.

And surprise, surprise! Santa had left a special present for Heathcliff!

"Yaaay!" thought Heathcliff. "I guess Christmas is for cats, too. Christmas is for *everybody!*"